If I Knew a Flamingo

Written and Illustrated by Karen Sutula

This book is dedicated to my children Nature and Alaska
and to all my nieces and nephews:
TJ, Brandon, Michael, Mattingly, Ava,
Avery, Cleo, Ashlyn, and Hailey.
I love you all so much!

I WOULD ASK HER WHERE DOES SHE GO,

WHEN THE SUN GOES DOWN

Does she like being lost in the crowd

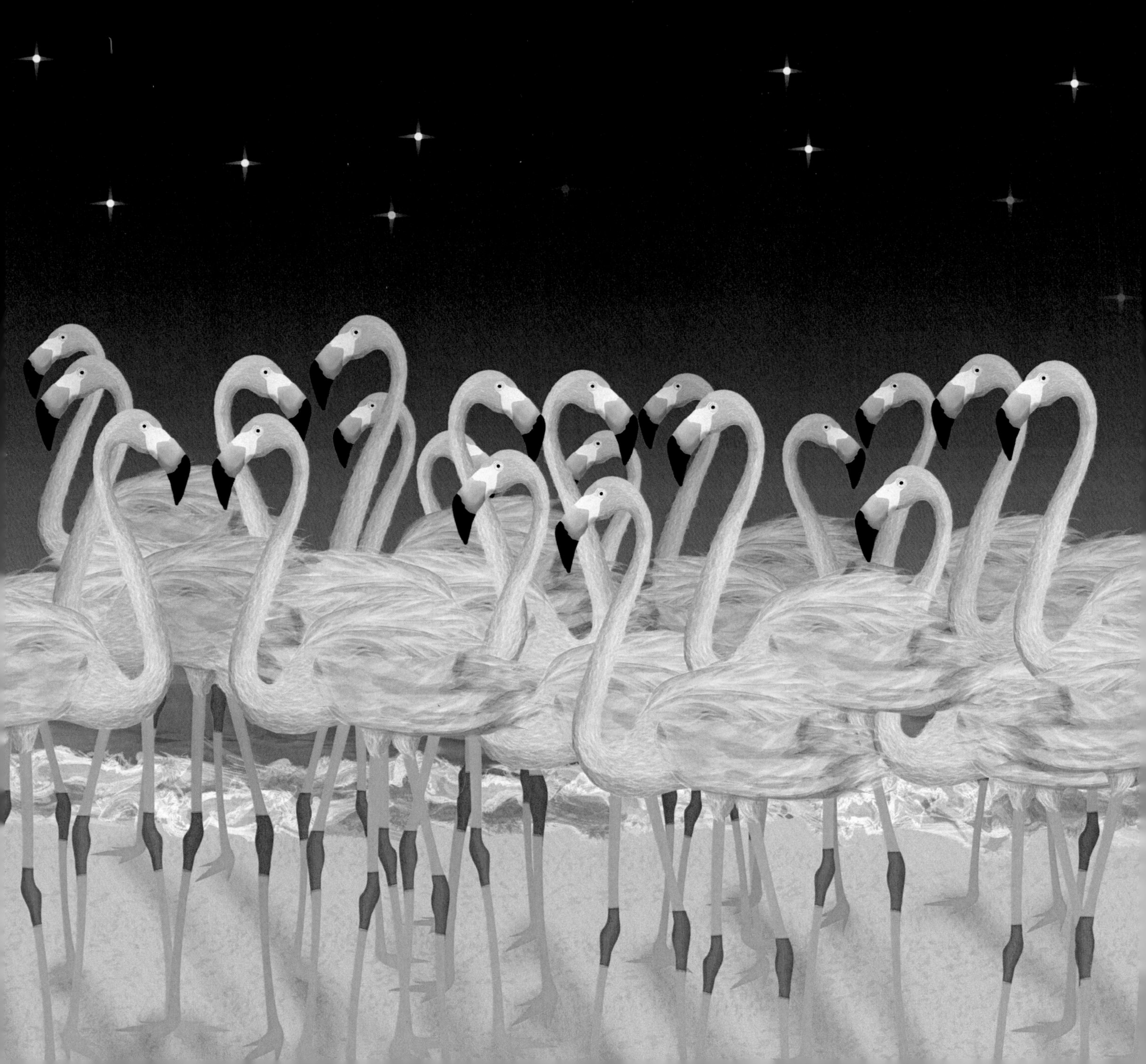

THAT FROM TIME TO TIME SHE VISITS FRIENDS NEARBY,

LIKE THE PEACEFUL ARMADILLO
WHO ALWAYS WEARS A SOMBRERO,

Or the nimble spider monkey
Who can sometimes be a little cranky,

Or the graceful puma
Who wants to learn to hula,

Or the baby tapir

WHO DREAMS OF BEING A GREAT RACER.

THEN THAT BEAUTIFUL PINK FLAMINGO
MIGHT JUST SAY AS THE DAWN BEGINS TO GLOW,

"GOODBYE, I REALLY MUST BE GOING.

THE MORNING LIGHT HAS CLEARLY STARTED SHOWING."

SADLY, I WOULD WATCH HER FLY AWAY,
AND VERY LOUDLY I WOULD SAY,

"Maybe next time you'll stop and visit me.
Then I will happily be